WILD HEART RANCH BOOKS
Published by Wild Heart Ranch Inc.
Wild Heart Ranch Books USA, 1385 Gulf Road, Suite 102, Point Roberts, WA 98281

Text copyright © 2005 by Dawn Van Zant.
Illustrations copyright © Alexander Levitas

Design and graphic realization by Evolutionary Imaging and Advertising Design
B1-1100 W. 6th Ave, Vancouver, BC, Canada

Library of Congress Catalog Card Number: 2005900058

Van Zant, Dawn
      Bradford and the Journey to the Desert of Lop

ISBN 0-9761768-2-3

Wild Heart Ranch Books

This book was printed in China

ISBN 0-9761768-2-3

90000

9 780976 176824

Bradford and the Journey to the Desert of Lop

This book is dedicated to Bradford Lawless, a true warrior at heart. His journey and his battle with cancer (Ewing's Sarcoma) became my inspiration to create this book and to tell the story of the wild camels, and the people of the Desert of Lop. It is my hope that through Brad, we can help save the camels as well as fund research to discover whether they hold a possible cure for cancer.

My mother, Evelyn, and my friend, Wayne Schiewe, were also instrumental in helping me understand the meaning of courage.

Please follow me on this journey of the heart

Written by Dawn Van Zant

Dawn is the founder of Wild Heart Ranch Inc., and author of its original stories, inspired by a love of nature. Her two children, Callan and Taylor, have always encouraged her writing and love of horses. Her father read her animal bedtime stories as a child and it instilled a desire to create and pass along her own stories.

Illustrated by Alexander Levitas

Alexander Levitas was born in the Uzbekistan, formerly known as Tashkent, where he studied at the Pedagogical High College. He worked as both a teacher and interior design artist before emigrating to Israel where he now lives and works on a kibbutz. Alex first began illustrating in 1994 and has lent his talents to more than 30 books. His illustrations can be found in a variety of historical literature, classical and young adult fiction in 4 different languages.

In loving memory of Brad:

Pediatric Cancer Support Group Resources Page

Ewing's Sarcoma Support Group Resources Page: http://www.cureourchildren.org/

Bradford and the Journey to the Desert of Lop

When the Sandman comes to visit you tonight, you need to listen closely as you close your eyes and drift off to sleep. He will tell you a story that you need to know. As he drops the soft grains of sand and dust once carried by the winds of the Gobi desert, you can hear the sand dunes whispering a bedtime story. It is a tale of the magic that lives in the desert, of buried ancient treasures, vanishing wild camels, forgotten people and the courage of a small, unlikely warrior destined to be their guardian.

The story tells of a mysterious, waterless land in the shape of a crescent moon surrounded by majestic mountains that guard some of the oldest secrets of all time. The land of wind and sun tells the tale of brave explorers, lost cities, treasures, and fossils buried beneath the golden sand.

Once an ancient inland sea, this desert holds the stories and bones of dinosaurs from eighty million years ago. If you let the desert wind dance across your face, you can hear the stories of how those dinosaurs first lived and then vanished.

The yellow-brown dust of the Gobi desert is carried in the winds to spread the story of lands once traveled by Marco Polo. He witnessed and heard the strange sights and sounds of the desert; the voices of spirits, the sounds of music, and the distant rumble of soldiers marching in the sand. Mysterious musical sounds rise from the vast dunes to welcome the few that dare to venture by.

The great silk road of long ago, once a busy path between east and west has all but vanished and reduced its remains to myth and lore. The bustling streets, wealthy cities full of gold, jewels and forgotten kings, lie submerged in the vast desert, waiting for the wind to expose them. Some say faithful desert gnomes guard the hidden treasures below.

The winds dance across the desert dunes, hiding Mummies of ancient kingdoms as they whisper secrets so old that time has forgotten them. Only the tiny grains of round stones know the stories of long ago.

It is a land few have traveled from beginning to end. There are places that man has never seen, where footprints have never been left behind. The borderlands are filled with vanishing wild animals; harbingers of fate. The last remaining wild camels on earth live in the Desert of Lop, hiding away from the world of man, waiting for a chosen one to tell their story and change their fate.

They search for the one who has courage enough to venture into the blazing heat, face the sand storms, and who can listen to the haunting sounds of the desert and not be afraid. The wild camels of the desert challenged the winds to travel the world to find this 'one'. A powerful dust storm gathered in the Gobi, and the cloud found its way to Alaska and then traveled down the coast of North America. The dust circled the planet once before falling from the sky. The tiny grains of sand, once walked upon by ancient warriors and kings, found their mark.

In a warm bed, an unsuspecting young boy, who could only walk in his dreams, awaited his destiny. This is the story of Bradford and his journey to the Desert of Lop. It is a story you must know.

The Sandman and the Magic Dust

Bradford lay in his bed, comforted by the warmth of his blue nightcap that his grandmother had made especially for him. It was sprinkled with stars and moons and had a gold tassel. He had lost a lot of weight from his cancer and the nightcap kept his head warm, so he could feel warm all over. He had asked for it one night before Christmas and knew exactly how he wanted it to look. It was an unusual request from a child, as no one really wears nightcaps anymore. But Brad was an unusual child, so nothing he said or did surprised his parents anymore.

He was sleeping in his extra large black t-shirt with silver lettering that simply said "WARRIOR." A friend had it made for him not too long ago at local t-shirt shop. It seemed to sum up who he was in a simple word. Brad felt stronger wearing it.

Brad always knew instinctively what he needed and was not afraid to ask for it. He had taken charge of his battle with cancer and fought valiantly for almost four years. His long necklace that held his cancer beads, were his badges of honor; each colored bead marking a different medical treatment or event, like when he lost his hair. It had all grown back, and now he loved to keep it long, shaggy and streaked.

When he was younger, he would plan mock battles and fight with his older sister. He would make weapons and swords out of anything he could find and practice with Danielle over and over again as he prepared for his destiny. His mother would shake her head, wondering why he wanted to fight, but later she would understand. He was in training for his battle.

Now as he lay in bed, in the middle of the family's transformed living room, he wished for the day when he could once again charge into battle like the true warrior he knew he was. The room was full of things he loved. Everyone who knew him and saw his courage brought him gifts. Every kind of stuffed animal imaginable was scattered around the room. There were pictures and cards from his friends at school taped to the walls. Photographs of his family, his favorite toys, video games, blankets, water glasses, and medicines were lined up on coffee tables, ledges and the fireplace mantle.

He had a TV in front of him, and every day he would watch Zorro and join him on his adventures, watching the heroic actions unfold. He watched the show over and over and it never lost its magic and power over him. Brad was studying, the best way he knew how, to be a hero too.

He imagined being Zorro as he tried to fall asleep. The room grew still as the Sandman came to bring him a good nights' sleep and dreams, sprinkling magic sand onto Bradford.

As he lay thinking in his bed, he felt a gentle presence in his room drift over him and it seemed as if something tiny and soft was falling on him, tickling his face. His big eyes opened and he pulled back his nightcap around his tousled hair. He could not see what was there but he challenged it.

"Who is there?" he demanded. The boy startled the Sandman. Children never knew he was there. For thousands of years he has come and gone unnoticed and never been questioned. "I said, 'who's there'!" he spoke again. The Sandman wondered with excitement if this small boy was the 'the one' he had traveled with the Gobi winds to find? He was such a frail young boy; he could not be the chosen one. But the sand had found its mark here in this room.

"I am the Sandman. I have come in search of a hero, the one chosen to travel the shifting sands in a quest of honor. Do you know of one? Do you know of a hero?" he asked, leading the boy to his answer.

"I know! I know everything!" Brad declared boldly. Underneath the covers Brad was really afraid of the voice in his room but he knew he could not show fear. 'A warrior never shows fear in the face of danger', he thought to himself. Thinking of Zorro, Brad's voice boomed from his bed "I am the chosen one!", and he reached for his toy sword.

The Sandman smiled an ancient smile. He looked at the boy wearing a warrior shirt and a blue nightcap, with eyes as large as the moon, and a body that was becoming a shadow of the strong, husky frame it used to be. He knew that Brad was the one.

"Are you ready for your journey?" he whispered to Brad. "Are you willing to travel the mysterious lands of the vast Gobi with me tonight? Can you walk with me in your dreams tonight and become the hero we are searching for? If you come, you will be as powerful and strong as your heart wills you. All you need is courage."

That was enough reason for Brad to go. He had the heart of warrior and he was born for adventure. More than anything, he wanted to be able to get out of his bed and walk again.

He had always loved camels for some reason, so he asked, "Do you think I will see camels in the Gobi?"

"The camels are waiting for you. They are the ones who have sent the winds to find you," smiled the Sandman triumphantly. Brad pondered the meaning of what the Sandman had said. Then a rush of excitement filled him.

Brad's eyes raced around the room searching for what he should take with him. He reached up and grabbed the Sandman's hand and felt himself get out of bed with renewed strength and power. He filled a bag with his cancer beads, to mark his trail in the desert so he would not get lost. He grabbed his Zorro video, a video game, hands full of treats, ginger molasses cookies, his favorite orange t-shirt, his brown kaki pants, runners, a baseball hat, his toothbrush, a picture of him and his sister, and a toy sword. He was ready to go.

He took one last look around the room and followed the wind, holding on to the Sandman's hand. He had no idea how long it took to find the desert. It could be minutes, or hours, or days.

He found himself falling to the soft sand below and gazing upon the vast dunes, mountains, steppes, and deep blue sky in front of him. The Sandman let go of his hand and watched the small boy walk towards his destiny, leaving behind the footprints of a hero in the warm sand.

The heat felt good and he felt welcomed by the Gobi. It seemed like the biggest place on earth, with no beginning and no end in sight.

"Where do I go?" he asked.

"This is your journey. In this magical dream, I can only follow and watch over you, but you must find your own path," said the Sandman.

Bradford looked all around at the wonders of the mysterious land and saw a large eagle soaring above him. "I will follow the eagle," he decided and the journey of the Desert of Lop began. A dark brown feather fell from the sky and he put it in his bag and felt the necklace touch his fingers. Brad took a small black bead off of his necklace to mark the beginning.

"The end of the Gobi is not the end of your journey," the wind whispered. The land called his name as he traveled through the hills and steppes, walking towards a distant barren land ahead. The wild eyes of the rare Gobi bear, the snow leopards, and desert wolves watched as he moved slowly away.

Herds of khulan, wild ancestors of the domestic ass, raced across the desert steppes, feeling the rush of excitement in the ground beneath.

The Wild Camels Appear

The heat wrapped around him and slowed him down. His small feet felt heavy. It was hard to breathe as the wind picked up dust that filled his eyes and nose. He stood still for a moment and listened. The singing dunes were calling to him. "Wait and they will come, wait quietly under the desert sun"; Brad closed his eyes and held out his arms as the wind danced around him. The soft beat of galloping hooves approached him. Brad could sense something near but his eyes were still filled with dust and they hurt when he tried to open them. So he waited. Then he felt something soft touch his hands.

As if by magic, the wind stopped, the dust settled, and the heat lifted its blanket. He opened his eyes and they were filled with the sight of a herd of wild camels - a bull, several females, and their young calves. The two humped shaggy camels appeared almost orange against the backdrop of the desert in the blazing sun. They had formed a circle around him and were kneeling on the desert sand. In the center, he slowly moved and looked deeply into their soft big eyes one by one. He felt that he knew these camels from a time long ago. As he turned slowly to his right, his eyes met with a female camel and he knew instinctively what she wanted. He walked gently towards her and climbed upon her back. Slowly, she rose fully upright, and the herd followed suit, one by one as if in a rhythmic dance.

The Sandman stood in awe at the beauty of the camels' graceful movements, and before the last camel stood, he climbed aboard his mount. Quietly, in a procession, one by one, the herd led by Brad and the female walked towards the sun. Quietness filled the air but there was a loud cry of purpose singing in the far off dunes. There was hope under the blazing sun.

As they marched along, Brad whistled a tune he did not know, but it danced through his heart to find its way out into the world. It was a song of the desert that only the dunes of long ago remembered. They rejoiced in his song, and the earth beneath the camels' hooves moved rhythmically to the beat. Then he began to sing.

"I know this land from whence I come
The land of desert and endless sun
I know my journey has just begun
I will walk my walk
Until my job is done"

The Sandman smiled and hummed along.

As night approached, the heat faded and the big sky filled with light. The yellow dunes and the deep blue sky turned a brilliant orange before the stars came. Brad was filled with wonder at the sight of all the orange and felt the magic of the desert energy all around him. Brad had always loved the color orange; he even dyed his hair bright orange before his first rounds of chemo.

A blanket of stars filled a sky that was endless, like the desert in front of him. The moon silhouetted the image of a small boy riding a camel through the desert night. He wore his nightcap filled with moons and stars, the tassel dancing in the wind and his sword at his side. The moon smiled. The marching came to a quiet stop, and the camels slowly lowered themselves and their passengers to the ground.

"Where will we sleep?" asked Brad. "Under the stars, in the circle of our new friends, on a bed of sand," whispered the Sandman.

It grew colder as the night fell. Brad snuggled in beside his camel and was not afraid of the desert night, and the desert knew it.

"Will my family be looking for me?" he asked. "Won't they be worried that I am gone?"

"Time has no place here in the desert. The desert does not allow time within its borders and if time were foolish enough to follow, it would be lost in the dunes" said the Sandman. "When your journey is done, you can return and they will not know how long you have been gone."

Brad felt stronger knowing his absence was not worrying his family. He sang himself to sleep.

"I will walk all day in the desert sun
I will walk my walk until my job is done
I will walk with friends one by one
I will walk my walk until my battle's won"

The desert sighed knowingly as he sang. The dunes sang this song with him, a song older than the bones that lay buried beneath the sand. It was ancient and new all at once.

When they awoke, the camels repeated their ritual of lowering themselves and carried their passengers in a knowing direction past steep dunes and gorges, to a hidden oasis and a fresh water spring. The cool, clear water appeared out of nowhere as if by a miracle. The camels filled themselves with water and so did Brad. He washed his face, took off his nightcap, and put it safely in his bag. He put on his baseball cap and smiled brightly.

Brad was seeing the desert as a magical place filled with singing dunes and blue skies. Whatever he needed seemed to appear before him. He saw nothing to fear in this place. As the winds exposed ancient bones in his path, he saw them as fascinating reminders of lives lived long ago, not as scary old bones and skulls.

He looked at the female that carried him. He decided to name her Judy, not really for any reason at all: he just decided that should be her name.

The Sandman asked him as they rested and drank: "So what do you like about camels?"

"Oh, just about everything." Brad smiled. "I also like turtles a lot."

As if the wind heard his voice, it picked up and shifted sand in front of him to show him the fossil of an ancient sea turtle. "Wow!" Brad said. "A turtle skeleton in the middle of desert; I wonder what else is buried here?"

"The sands of time have hidden many stories and treasures that will unfold to you when you are ready to know them. You will see the world is smaller than you thought, in many ways, and much larger than you have dreamed, in others. Everything you need to know is here in this desert. It is barren and it is full." The Sandman paused for a moment and then spoke quietly, "It is in the places hidden from man that we find the answers: in the sky, the ocean and the desert."

At times, Brad thought that the way the Sandman spoke in riddles was quite strange, but his company was more than welcome on this adventure. He wondered what this day would bring.

The People of Lop Nor

Brad could hear what he thought were people singing off in the distance. Slowly, a group of people with beautiful round faces, wearing colorful hats and multi-colored clothes appeared. Some were walking and others were riding donkeys.

The people of the wind and sun joined his herd of camels. They looked at Brad and smiled. He could not understand what they said, but he thought he heard the word Lop. 'Well, they aren't going to come here and lop off my head while I am asleep,' he thought. He reached for his toy sword, and looked for the largest of the group to challenge to a duel. He posed like Zorro and drew a letter B in the sand. The wind picked up and blew the dust into the face of his opponent. The people looked in amazement then began to laugh.

Brad was not sure if they were laughing at him or with him, but he felt safer.

The Sandman watched quietly and then spoke to Brad. "They are the Uighurs, people that live near the Desert of Lop. They left their farms and villages, and have traveled to find you and bring you to their home. We are not near their homes yet: we have many miles to travel. Now that they too have found you, like the camels, they will walk with you one by one."

"They were once great warriors," he continued. "There is a legend that tells the story of how their ancestors came from the daughter of one of the Hun rulers and a wolf." The Sandman knew this was intriguing the small boy, and stirring his imagination.

Brad loved the idea of traveling with the Sandman, wild camels, and a band of warriors descended from wolves. This was like a real life video game adventure for him. He felt exhilarated and alive under the hot desert sun. The cancer was left far behind him in a distant memory, and had lost its power over him in this mysterious place. Here, he felt strong and whole, but the Uighurs could see the ghosts of a familiar sickness, like those of many children in their village. It gave them great hope to see Brad strong, brave and able, leading them to their destiny. He sang again.

> "I will walk all day in the desert sun
> I will walk my walk until my job is done
> I will walk with friends one by one
> I will walk my walk until my battle's done"

The camels swayed to and fro, the Uighurs danced and sang along. The Sandman watched and smiled quietly.

Brad was not sure what battle lay ahead, but he felt he could face it as his army marched with him into the desert.

The weather was perfect this day, with no wind to slow them down. They passed over large sand dunes, leaving their long trail of hoof prints and footprints. Every so often, Brad would drop a bead to mark his path. He knew the sand could easily bury his single bead, but it gave him comfort to drop them in the desert sand as they marched along.

He looked down occasionally, and would spot a lizard scurrying across the sand and stones. Once he saw what he thought was part of a dinosaur egg rising from the grains. He did not stop to look; it was enough for him to know it was there. Some secrets should remain secret, he thought.

The Sandman called to him through the wind, "Would you like to feel your camel run? Do you want to chase the soft desert breeze?"

Brad was filled with a rush of excitement and all at once the herd galloped off. It was one of the best moments of his life. The herd slowed down as the desert sand softened and deepened beneath them. They walked slowly, waiting for the Uighurs. Together they traveled with a timeless rhythm of life.

"Why don't they ride the camels too?" asked Brad. "Because the wild camels did not invite them to", stated the Sandman. "Can wild things make choices the tame cannot?" He asked calmly.

"Another one of your riddles?" smirked Brad.

"No," the Sandman sighed as he followed the boy, "it is just a question from an old one that has witnessed many wild things vanish or lose their spirit in our midst."

Guardians of Ancient Tombs

The camels led the gathering of warriors through two more days and nights of easy travel. It was hot and tiring, but the winds were quiet and made passage swift. They passed through springs and stopped to rest, drink and eat. The Uighurs tried to tell Brad their stories and drew pictures in the sand telling him of their mysterious desert lives and history. They drew winding rivers, pictures of many warriors, battles won and lost, and other things he did not recognize.

They showed how, long ago they came from another place and how they came to live in the desert land they called their home. He could not really understand what they said, but he sensed a long and troubled history of warriors in his presence. Still, they carried themselves with a desert pride that the camels shared. It was a pride of survival. Brad understood the meaning of it as he thought about the beads in his bag.

"Lop Nor", they said softly and sketched out what looked like a map. Then they designed what looked like a flag blowing in the wind - with a single moon and a star on it. It made Brad think of his nightcap and he pulled it out for them to see. They looked in awe at the blue cap with moons and stars on it.

Who was this small boy with big blue eyes who shared the faint but familiar signs of their villagers' illness? Who was this brave boy that marched like a warrior as their ancestors did? Who was under the blue nightcap with moons and stars that blew softly in the night wind, reminding them of a forgotten flag?

The Sandman watched from a distance as the circle of fate closed in and the boy's destiny became clearer.

They traveled past the dunes towards a valley. The camels became uneasy and could smell danger in the wind. The desert called out a haunting cry for help as a white jeep trampled over the land below, and sped off with priceless treasures.

When Brad and his band of warriors reached the place from which the thieves had fled; sadly, he could see what had happened. An ancient tomb had been raided and smashed once the thieves had taken what they came for. Bones and murals were scattered all over, and precious silk fabrics were almost destroyed. Lost threads of history unraveled with the silk below them. Brad could see pieces of a mural with two camels on it, one golden and one silver. His curiosity rose.

The Sandman came from behind and looked down at the tomb. "Long ago, camels were symbols of power" he spoke. "I know." Brad declared. He whistled to Judy and led the charge with his camel galloping off to chase the raiders in their jeep. "Mine is powerful today," he cheered.

The rest followed him in pursuit of the thieves. The desert won its battle that day as the jeep approached a dune too deep to cross, and too great to go around.

Brad, the camels, and the Uighurs surrounded them and confronted the "desert rats" that showed no respect for the sacred tombs.

Brad circled his sword in the air at the two cowardly thieves who were yelling in a language he did not understand. They could not believe what they were seeing, but were afraid to challenge the strange boy with all of the wild camels and Uighurs standing at his side. Three of the Uighurs quietly took the contents of the jeep and walked softly back towards the tombs.

For a moment in time, the east and west were joined once again on the Silk Road, through the boy from the west and the clan of the east, uniting in a common cause.

"What should we do with these robbers?" asked Brad, turning to the Sandman. "Feed them to the desert gnomes? Or how about feeding these rats to the desert snakes?!"

The camels snorted and decided the fate of the two thieves. The camels chased the thieves further into the barren desert on foot, to places men may venture, but of which few return to tell.

That night, the sand dunes sang beautiful songs to Brad and the Uighurs, while further away the strangers were haunted by wild spirits screaming from the dunes; driving the thieves to madness.

Brad wore his nightcap and pulled it down over his small head. He went soundly to sleep as he relived every moment of the battle that day. As he felt the warmth of Judy beside him, he was reminded of sleeping beside his mom on the many nights he was sick. He missed his family, but knew he was not yet ready to return.

Learning to Wait

In the morning, a yellow storm started to blow. The march of the dust storm was more ominous than an army. The relentless sandstorm seemed to be filling up the whole sky above, sending messages of its existence out to the world. Brad had never seen a storm like this. The desert people had seen them many times before, and so had the wild camels. Brad's nightcap found a new purpose as he pulled it down over his face. Gold dust from the Gobi roared into the sky and found its way around the globe, while the band of warriors waited it out.

Visibility was zero, making travel impossible. The desert held them captive as it blew away the dust to places where it may not have been wanted.

Brad could feel Judy, the shaggy golden camel, huddling around him to protect him from the storm. She had her back to the storm and lay her head and neck down on the sand. He was not afraid as he waited with her. He understood the desert was teaching him new lessons. It was teaching him to respect its power and how to wait for its calm. The warriors spent the day and night learning the lesson.

Lop Nor

As they awoke, the desert in China's far west, known by its Uighur name of Lop Nor, was suddenly within their reach. Yellow-gray sand and clay sprinkled with gravel, painted a mysterious path in the distance. Brad was amazed at the Gobi and how it changed so dramatically as he traveled it.

Brad took off his nightcap and routinely put it in his bag. He reached inside and pulled out the photograph of him sitting with his sister, Danielle.

He showed the Uighurs and they all smiled. "Danielle" he said, and they nodded and tried to say her name. The young man sitting beside him said "Kashi", pointing to him. In his language he had declared, "I am strong man of the desert."

Then Brad introduced himself "Bradford, the warrior". One by one they told him their names.

They offered him breakfast; bread sprinkled with poppy seeds and Uighur bagels. They were delicious and Brad felt like he was at his favorite bakery instead of in the middle of desert.

He sat with his new friends and wondered quietly who these people were and why they had come looking for him, just as the wild camels had. And what was Lop Nor? This, he asked aloud without realizing it.

"The Desert of Lop", said the Sandman, "the home of the vanishing wild camels that live on the north edge of the desert. It is a land of clay and sand, of wild asses, ravens and eagles soaring above a barren land. On the fringes, live the Uighurs and the desert nomads. Bad things have happened in the Desert of Lop, secret things. Some nights the dunes in Lop Nor weep, trying to forget what they have witnessed."

Brad's eyes grew bigger. "What did they see? What secret things happened in the Desert of Lop?"

"You will know that soon, and also the reason that you are here. Very soon, just follow your path."

Brad looked above him and the eagle appeared in the sky above him, as it did in the beginning of his journey. "I will follow the eagle," and he and Judy marched ahead.

"I will walk all day in the desert sun
I will walk my walk until my job is done
I will walk with friends one by one
I will walk my walk until my battle's done"

The eagle flew towards the cliffs in the distance. Carved out of the cliffs on the fabled Silk Road were ancient caves with murals. They were left to remind us of forgotten merchants, travelers and their camel caravans. The camels walked towards the blooming flowers and the green trees of the oasis for a much needed rest, leaving behind the dry hot dust and stones of the desert. The Desert of Lop would be a hot, tiring journey for all.

The caves filled Brad with awe and serenity. The Sandman told him they were holy caves carved out by Buddhists, filled with paintings and statues to remind us of a time of harmony long ago.

The Mushroom Shadows

As they entered the Desert of Lop and the landscape changed, Brad found himself filled with an eerie sense of sadness. The sun reflected the sadness on the faces of his desert friends. The desert cast shadows across the sand that looked like giant mushroom clouds. The wind shifted, but the shadows followed them. The Uighurs seemed undaunted as they traveled along.

The mushroom clouds painted on the sand grew in number and in size. The sand and clay seemed to turn from golden to gray.

The camels came to a stop, as if they had found a clear water spring, but instead drank from a salty slush. Brad did not understand. This place was not like the land of the day before. And how could the camels drink this water? Surely no one expected him to drink it? To his relief, the Uighurs did not drink either.

As the day went on and they got closer to their home, the rhythm of the donkeys, the camels and the Uighurs changed from a defiant march, to a mournful walk. Brad felt the world change around and beneath him. He thought the end of the march would be joyful, not sad. But the desert was full of mysteries and he had learned not to question, but to wait for answers.

They saw desert nomads in the distance, Kazakh herdsmen that live on the fringes of Lop Nor, traveling with their domestic camels. Brad wondered if they were different from the wild camels he was traveling with. All he knew about this wild herd that had found him in the middle of the desert, was that they seemed to have an air of magic about them that could not be explained in mere words.

As they passed through the borders of the desert, they approached the Uighur country. He saw women and the children in brightly colored scarves, donkeys, carts and a quiet sense of the world awaiting him.

That night the Uighurs welcomed Brad with warm noodles and meat for dinner. He and the Sandman ate happily, while the herd of wild camels waited outside the village. Brad looked around after dinner and could see a familiar sadness and pain in the faces, even the ones covered with long beards. This place was filled with a familiar sickness, one he knew too well. He had seen it too many times at the hospital, in the faces of other children. He had also seen it reflected in the faces of families. There was a cancer in this place.

Why had the Sandman made him travel for days in the sun and wind, facing danger to end up in a place that was full of a sickness he was happy to leave behind in his small bed? How could cancer have followed him this far, to a land that was hidden away from most of the world?

The Sandman read his thoughts and looked at the boy. He walked towards him with the truth in his hand. It was single grain of sand.

"Take this, hold it gently, and listen to its story," he whispered.

The tiny grain had a large tale to tell. It told Brad the story of the mushroom clouds. The desert watched a clear blue sky become painted with a brilliant pinkish white flash. Then, a light blue nimbus cloud appeared. It stretched to touch the ground and raised dust and sand all around it. The cloud rose upward and then seemed to drop a million grains of sickness from the sky. The desert air was filled with a powerful and unnatural heat that made the earth shake in fear. The grains of sickness in the sky fell and found their marks upon an unsuspecting land below.

The tiny grain of sand repeated the story over and over to him again until it had told him the story over forty times. Brad was only nine, but he was wise beyond his years. After all, he knew everything. Brad now understood the mushroom shadows that had followed him through Lop Nor.

Brad walked back to the Uighurs and walked through the village, staring into their faces one by one. He took out his cancer beads and placed them in the hands of the children marked by the mushroom clouds. He shared his badges of honor with them to mark their story.

He looked around for a hospital but saw none. He looked for a doctor in their midst, but none appeared. He saw people in the bazaar stalls selling dried snakes, lizards, bark, and plants to the sick. The potions were all they had. Brad remembered how the nurses and doctors and his family had watched over him every day of his illness. Brad looked at the faces of the children and wished for a miracle. The desert winds picked up his wish and carefully sent it to its destination.

The wild camels wandering through the desert night heard the boy's wish as the wind whispered into their ears. The wild camels, with a history as old as the secrets of the Silk Road, walked towards the small boy. They were the last of their kind, a vanishing breed, fighting a battle for survival, preyed upon by wolves, gold miners, thieves and hunters. But the mushroom clouds had not found their mark on the wild herds: the desert sands would not allow it.

The Sandman smiled as destiny completed its circle. "The desert is barren and it is full," he sighed.

The Miracle of the Camels

Brad saw the camels walking towards him and it reminded him of their first meeting. He had known from the first moment they appeared that they were magical. They walked softly through the sand with grace. Even with their shaggy coats, covered in clay and dust from rolling in the desert, they were beautiful. He loved them in the deepest part of his heart. He was connected to them in a mysterious way, which only the desert understood.

He was reminded of what the Sandman had said about wild things and about choices. He knew the camels chose him.

As they neared, he was struck by the thought that these camels living in the same desert land as the Uighurs, showed no signs of the mushroom sickness. They were healthy and so were their babies. The camels carried no signs of cancer. Cancer could not disguise itself or hide from the small warrior. He knew it too well and demanded its honesty.

He had learned about cancer during his own battle with it. He understood a cancer cell was just calling to an ancient memory, back to the beginning of time, on how to survive in a world with less oxygen. Cancer cells were just trying to live. Everything was just trying to live, here also in this place so far away from home.

Maybe these camels, knew the secrets of life. They were healthy and alive against all odds. They too were warriors. Maybe these ships of the desert were carrying the answer for the Uighurs and the children of the world like him. He remembered the Sandman telling him, "It is in the places hidden from man that we find the answers - in the sky, the ocean and the desert".

"What if these camels are the answer? We can't let them vanish in the desert with their secrets.   Sands - bury your gold and hide your silver and jewels, but don't let the camels' magic be lost here too!" he cried out to the desert.

He picked up a hand full of sand and let the grains sift through his small fingers and closed his eyes. He asked the desert sand to tell him the story of the wild camels.

The sand told him that these camels were the last remnants of the wild herds from long ago. Their ancestors had come from North America on the Bering Strait land bridge almost four million years ago. They carried the history of times forgotten. The desert had chosen to save the last of these wild camels. These camels had learned to survive by drinking salt water, when no other camels could; had escaped the dark sickness dropped in the desert, when man could not; and had learned to live in the forgotten lands of clay and sand. Was it the saltwater, was it the clay, or was it something in the wild camels' genes that spared them? Or was it just the wish of the desert winds?

Brad now understood his quest. He must find a way to tell the world about this place, its people, and save the last herds of wild camels from vanishing in our midst. He must unravel their secret and their truth and share it with the world. Some day their magic and power would spread across the world with the desert winds. He promised himself he would not return home until it was done. Brad sang his song to the camels.

"I will walk all day in the desert sun
I will walk my walk until my job is done
I will walk with friends one by one
I will walk my walk until my battle's won"

"The end of the Gobi is not the end of your journey," the wind whispered. Brad walked towards Judy and whispered back to the wind, "I know". He dropped another cancer bead in the soft sand and marked his fate. He smiled as the desert sun painted his world orange.

The Journey

So when the sandman comes tonight, you need to listen to the story of the Gobi dust, because in every story there is a grain of truth. The truth is that the wild camels, the Uighurs and the unlikely young hero do exist. Their story is Brad's story. They chose him to tell their truth because he has the courage of a warrior. One small boy with cancer can change the world if you listen.

So close your eyes as you drift off to sleep and imagine him riding through the desert on the back of Judy the camel, wearing his warrior shirt, his blue night cap with moons and stars flying like a flag in the wind, and waving his sword. He is riding through your dreams to find your heart, because it alone can hear the truth of the Desert of Lop.

Saving Wild Camels

Sponsor a Wild Bactrian Camel: A female baby camel, Judy, was adopted for Bradford and is now living at The Wild Camel Protection Foundation

"Scientists have every reason to think a detailed study of the immune system of the wild Bactrian camel will yield scientific discoveries which will be of benefit to the whole of mankind"

The Wild Camel Protection Foundation, a United Kingdom registered charity, with Jane Goodall as its patron, was established in 1997. It is also registered in the USA as a non-profit organization. The sole aim of the Wild Camel Protection Foundation is to protect the critically endangered wild Bactrian camel (Camelus bactrianus ferus) and its habitat in the fragile and unique desert ecosystems in the Gobi and Gashun Gobi deserts in North West China and South West Mongolia.

Now Critically Endangered - Will it survive?

The wild Bactrian camel, the remarkable ancestor of all domestic camels, lives in three separated habitats in China, and one in Mongolia. In 2002 , the wild Bactrian camel was listed by the IUCN as "critically endangered" following years of pressure from the Wild Camel Protection Foundation. There are approximately 600 surviving in China and 350 in Mongolia, making them rarer and more endangered than the giant panda.

Evolutionary History

The wild Bactrian camel has a special place in evolutionary history. The wild Bactrian camels in China and Mongolia are the remnants of herds which crossed from North America on the Bering Strait land bridge 3 - 4 million years ago. Some Bactrian camels were domesticated 4,000 years ago, but the wild Bactrian camels in the Gashun Gobi (Lop Nur) area, avoided domestication and are now genetically different from the domestic Bactrian camels. Moreover, research has shown that in the embryonic stage, one-humped, dromedary camels have a small second hump that does not develop further. This suggests that the ancestors of all camels on earth looked like the wild Bactrian camels today.

DNA Testing

Samples of skin taken from the remains of dead Bactrian camels have been sent to scientists for genetic DNA testing. The results have been remarkable. Each skin sample has shown two or three distinct genetic differences to the domestic Bactrian camel and a 3% base difference.

More Info: The wild Bactrian camel has adapted and managed to survive in an area of China, the Gashun Gobi which was for 45 years, a nuclear tests site. In spite of this, the wild Bactrian camel survived the effects of radiation and appeared to be breeding naturally. In some areas in the absence of fresh water it had also to adapt to drinking salt water slush. Domestic Bactrian camels will not drink salt water.